SCORPION MAN

SCORPION MAN

Exploring the World of Scorpions

LAURENCE PRINGLE

PHOTOGRAPHS BY

GARY A. POLIS

CHARLES SCRIBNER'S SONS • NEW YORK
Maxwell Macmillan Canada • Toronto
Maxwell Macmillan International
New York • Oxford • Singapore • Sydney

Grateful acknowledgment is made to the following for the use of photographs: Galina Fet for the photograph of Gary Polis (cover); Philip Brownell (frontispiece); Robert Mitchell (page 14, top left); Maria Polis (page 29); Stephen Polis (page 33); and Sharon Lee Polis (page 39).

Charles Scribner's Sons Books for Young Readers
Macmillan Publishing Company, 866 Third Avenue, New York, NY 10022

Maxwell Macmillan Canada, Inc.
1200 Eglinton Avenue East, Suite 200, Don Mills, Ontario M3C 3N1

Macmillan Publishing Company is part of the
Maxwell Communication Group of Companies.

First edition   10   9   8   7   6   5   4   3   2   1
Printed in Hong Kong on recycled paper

Library of Congress Cataloging-in-Publication Data
Pringle, Laurence P.
Scorpion man : exploring the world of scorpions /
Laurence Pringle ; photographs by Gary A. Polis. — 1st ed.
p.   cm.   Includes bibliographical references (p.   ) and index.
ISBN 0-684-19560-7
1. Scorpions—Juvenile literature.   2. Scorpions—Research—California—Juvenile literature.
3. Polis, Gary A., date—Juvenile literature.
[1. Scorpions.   2. Polis, Gary A., date.   3. Biologists.]   I. Polis, Gary A., date, ill.
II. Title.
QL458.7.P75   1994   595.4'6—dc20   93-34936
SUMMARY: A photographic account of the work of a
wildlife biologist who specializes in scorpions.

CONTENTS

ONE

Becoming Scorpion Man

It was a moonless desert night, lit only by the ancient light of stars. Rodents scurried about, searching for seeds. A great horned owl called.

Gary Polis stood in the dark, enjoying the skyful of stars and the sounds of life stirring in the cool desert air. Then he flicked on his camping lantern. It emitted "black light"—ultraviolet light that is not visible to human eyes. As Gary Polis shone the light in a circle, he saw creatures giving off a bluish glow in the dark.

The bodies of scorpions reflect ultraviolet light. As Gary turned slowly he counted the scorpions. "One, two, three." Some stood still. "Eleven, twelve, thirteen." Some were on the move. "Eighteen, nineteen, twenty."

Being alone in the dark and surrounded by twenty scorpions would cause many people to scream in terror. Gary Polis relished the moment.

Exposed to ultraviolet light, a sand scorpion glows in the dark.

"I feel lucky," he says, "to have a career that brings me to wild deserts to study scorpions, which I feel are some of the earth's most fascinating animals."

For more than twenty years Gary Polis has observed scorpions in the deserts of the United States, Mexico, Australia, and Africa. He is considered an international expert on these venomous creatures. And yet, as a child, a teenager, and even as a college graduate, he never dreamed that he would become known as "scorpion man."

The second of six children, Gary was born in California in 1946. The Polis kids were raised in the San Fernando Valley, then mostly an area of fields and orchards. Gary remembers going on hikes led by his older brother, Dennis. He liked to turn over rocks and boards to look for lizards and other creatures. Recalling those days, he smiles and says, "I didn't know it was biology."

Family camping trips led to Yellowstone and other national parks, but Gary's favorite place was only about twenty-five miles from home: the rock-strewn Pacific beach at Malibu. He loved to explore there at low tide, finding starfish, flat worms, and sometimes octopuses.

At the age of ten, Gary recalls, he put on a combination circus and zoo show in the family garage. Catfish, bullfrogs, snakes, and lizards were on display. However, catching and studying wild animals was just one of Gary's interests. He played baseball, basketball, and other sports. He also read voraciously.

"Between the fifth and eighth grades, I read every science fiction book in our public library," Gary says. "My mother certainly influenced me; she reads and reads. And on our family trips and in everyday life, she expressed a sense of wonder and a love of knowledge."

Gary's father was a machinist in the aircraft industry who rose to become a plant superintendent. His commitment to work and

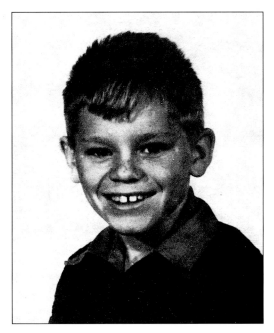

Gary Polis in the first grade.

his love of sports also influenced Gary and the other Polis children. Both parents earned college degrees when they were in their forties.

Gary, however, was not exactly a model student in the Roman Catholic parochial schools he attended: "I was hyperactive and felt bored, so I made wisecracks, played practical jokes, spent a lot of time in detention, and worked hard only when I wanted to. At the same time, I was voted 'most polite' by my classmates. I was the kind of student that teachers both love and hate."

In his junior year of high school Gary began to study more and to earn high grades; he aimed to attend college and needed to get scholarship aid. He graduated from high school in 1964 and entered Loyola University (now Loyola Marymount University) in Los Angeles. "I had no idea about what to major in," Gary recalls, "and chose biology because of all the fun I had outdoors, especially exploring tide pools at Malibu. I discovered that I enjoyed studying philosophy, so eventually I had twin majors, of philosophy and biology."

At Loyola Gary joined a fraternity and played a lot of sports. He enjoyed most of his classes but still had no clear idea of what he would do after graduation from college. After graduation in 1969, Gary became a science teacher. Beginning in the Watts area of eastern Los Angeles, he taught science to junior high and high school students. In 1972 students at El Camino Real High School in the San Fernando Valley voted Gary Polis "teacher of the year."

While teaching, Gary continued to study biology by taking night courses at UCLA (University of California at Los Angeles). On weekends and during vacations he often camped and explored wild areas with friends.

It was on one of those trips, in the spring of 1972, that he saw his first scorpion: "Beginning as a little kid I've turned over rocks and other objects to see what lived underneath. This time, in the Santa Monica Mountains, I turned over an abandoned oil drum and there was a scorpion. In mortal fear I backpedaled so fast I fell down! Later on, when I learned more about scorpions, I figured out that the species I saw was absolutely harmless."

That fall Gary began attending graduate school at the University of California at Riverside. It was considered the best place to study desert biology, and Gary was becoming increasingly fascinated by deserts. At Riverside Gary was a teaching assistant, took further science courses himself, and also searched for a subject to investigate. He considered a study of desert plants or of lizards.

In April 1973 a meeting in a hallway changed the focus of his studies—and the course of his life. Gary met Dr. Roger Farley, a neurobiologist at the university. (Neurobiology is the study of animal nervous systems.) Dr. Farley was not a field biologist, but he was looking for a graduate student who was. He felt that Gary Polis might be the right person for a new research project.

On a desert research area, Dr. Farley explained, there was a population of scorpions about which nothing was known. "Why don't you come out for a look?" he urged.

Scorpions? Gary knew very little about them and discovered, as he searched through scientific journals and books, that not much *was* known about them. Scorpions hide by day and are active at

In the early 1970s Gary Polis explored deserts and shores in Mexico with friends Larry Pomeroy and Ken Sculteure.

night, so they were thought to be difficult to observe. Most scorpion studies had been done in laboratories. Those biologists who had worked in natural habitats found scorpions by looking under rocks and other objects on the ground. They had little chance of learning about the many scorpion species that live in burrows.

In 1968, however, an article in *Bioscience* pointed out that already-mentioned characteristic of scorpions: They glow under ultraviolet light. Roger Farley had obtained ultraviolet (black-light) bulbs. Gary Polis set out to use this light to find and observe scorpions in their natural surroundings.

On an April night in 1973 he drove to the study area near Palm Springs, California. Exploring a large sand dune, shining the black light about, he saw scores of scorpions. "I soon discovered that scorpions were a great research subject. The black light made them visible, there were a lot of them, and they usually killed and ate their food right out in the open.

"Since so little was known about scorpions, I felt that whatever I did with them would yield some useful information."

The Windy Point dunes—where Gary Polis began to study scorpions.

TWO

A Deadly Reputation

Say *scorpion* to most people, and they will picture a small desert-dwelling animal, its curved tail tipped with a deadly stinger.

This description fits some scorpions, but it is about as accurate as saying that all humans are lawyers who live in cities. Less than 2 percent—about twenty-five of fifteen hundred known scorpion species—have venom that can kill people. And scorpions live not only in deserts but also in jungles, grasslands, caves, along seashores, and high on mountains.

Overall, scorpions are far more varied and much less dangerous than people imagine. Still, throughout history the few poisonous species have killed many people. As a result, in many cultures the scorpion is a symbol of evil and death. In the 1991 book he edited, *The Biology of Scorpions,* Gary Polis wrote, "The scorpion has appeared repeatedly in religious cults of ancient and modern history as an agent of the night, the devil, or the gods of the underworld."

Even though he knows how to handle scorpions safely, Gary Polis chooses not to study any deadly species. There are no accurate figures of deaths caused by scorpions worldwide, but estimates

A desert scorpion in its defensive position, ready to sting.

range from three thousand to five thousand victims a year. Medicines called antivenins can now save lives, but scorpions are still a major health hazard in parts of India, Africa, South America, and Mexico.

Just one deadly species lives in the United States. Its range extends from Mexico into Arizona and southern Utah. All other scorpions that live in the United States (and one species found also in southern Alberta and British Columbia, Canada) have poison stings that are no worse than those of honeybees or wasps. "I have been stung seven times by scorpions," Gary Polis says, "and the pain was never bad enough to make me stop what I was doing."

A scorpion's stinger is located at the tip of its tail. The tail whips forward in a split second to jab a victim and inject venom.

Just one scorpion species with a deadly sting lives in parts of the southwestern United States.

Chemists have discovered that scorpion venoms are a mixture of up to thirty neurotoxins (poisons that affect the nervous system). Each toxin is effective against different organisms, for example, insects, mice, and spiders.

Scorpions sting to defend themselves or to get food. However, many species rely more on their front claws, or pedipalps, than on venom for defense and food capture. "The bigger a scorpion's claws," says Gary Polis, "the less dangerous its venom. Avoid scorpions that have thin little, forcepslike pedipalps. These claws can't be very good for grabbing and crushing prey, so their presence is a warning that their owners have powerful poisons. In fact all of the most deadly scorpions, in the family Buthidae, have slender pedipalps."

Growing numbers of biologists have become fascinated with scorpions. "When you talk about scorpions, you tend to use a lot of words like 'the only known example,' 'the first,' 'the largest,' " says Gary Polis. "It's just one gee-whiz fact after another."

Scorpions are arachnids, related to spiders, mites, and ticks. All arachnids have eight legs while insects have six. Other arachnids include wind scorpions, false scorpions, and whip scorpions, also called vinegarroons. Despite their names, none of these creatures is a true scorpion.

Fossils of "water scorpions" have been found that are about 450 million years old. Some measured ten feet long. Some early land-dwelling scorpions were three feet long. All of these giant scorpions died out, but scorpions have been a remarkably successful and diverse group on land for the past 325 million years. They thrived before, during, and after the dinosaurs.

Today's scorpions resemble the body plan of their ancient ancestors. They all look generally alike. The smallest scorpion, a half inch long, lives on Caribbean islands. The largest, eight inches

A museum display shows a three-foot-long scorpion, known from fossils formed many millions of years ago.

long, lives in tropical Africa. Overall, scorpions are big creatures—the larger scorpion species are bigger than nearly all arachnids, insects, and other animals without backbones (invertebrates). In fact they are bigger than many lizards, rodents, frogs, and other vertebrates (animals with backbones).

Scorpions live on all major land masses except Antarctica. They thrive in many habitats. Some species are found right along ocean shores, where the tides carry in an abundance of food. Other species spend most of their lives in trees; an Australian scorpion that lives in pines has been found more than one hundred twenty feet above the ground.

Several kinds of scorpions live in caves. One of these was discovered more than a half mile below the surface. And still other species are mountain dwellers. They are found on ten thousand-foot-tall mountains in the southwestern United States. Some species live under snow-covered stones at even higher elevations in the Himalayas and Andes.

"Scorpions," says Gary Polis, "are not distributed randomly within a habitat. Rather, particular species are normally found in specific microhabitats. For example, in North America there are scorpions that live only in sand and others that live only on rock.

"The bodies, tails, and pedipalps of rock-dwelling scorpions are long and flat, adapted for slipping into cracks and crevices. Sand dwellers, on the other hand, are adapted for travel in loose sand. They have very long hairs that stick out from their legs. These and long claws allow the scorpions to walk on loose sand without sinking."

While some scorpions live only in certain habitats, many others are more "plastic," able to inhabit a variety of environments. One example is the scorpion species that lives on Socorro Island off the coast of Baja California in Mexico. It is found in jungle, heavy

The diversity of scorpions includes blind cave species (top, left), *one whose flat body enables it to slip easily under rocks and into crevices* (right), *and a sand-dwelling species from Africa* (below).

brush, rocky terrain, and sand, and also on the ground, in vegetation, and near the surf.

Scorpions are rather primitive, ancient animals, but are highly successful. Biologists are curious about the reasons for their success. One is their sense organs. Of all animals, scorpion eyes are the most sensitive to low levels of light. They can navigate using shadows cast by starlight. "Star shadows," says Gary Polis, "are probably as bright to scorpions as sun shadows are to people."

Sensitive hairs on the pedipalps of some scorpions detect air movements, including those caused by an insect flying nearby. These scorpions reach and grab prey out of the air. Some scorpions also have slitlike organs on their legs that detect vibrations in the ground caused by insects or other animals walking or burrowing several feet away.

Scorpions are tough. They endure extreme cold and heat. In deserts scorpions withstand temperatures several degrees higher than spiders, insects, and many other creatures. When above ground one way they accomplish this is called "stilting"—standing as tall as possible on their eight legs, lifting their bodies off the hot ground surface. Desert species also get along on very little water. They may never drink, because their liquid needs are met by water within the bodies of animals they eat.

Most scorpions don't travel far. They sit and wait for prey to come to them. So they don't "burn" much energy. All of their physical and chemical processes for maintaining life—their metabolism—operate at a low level. In fact, scorpions have some of the lowest rates of animal metabolism ever recorded. According to laboratory studies, scorpions have a lower metabolism than growing carrot or radish roots!

"You might think of scorpions as the champion 'couch potatoes' of all animals," says Gary Polis, "but this lack of activity helps them survive. They can live without food for over a year. And they may live for as long as twenty-five years. This is longer than any arachnid or insect, and also longer than many birds and mammals."

In mating and reproduction, scorpions are also remarkable creatures. They mate for the first time when two to six years old, depending on the species. Males usually seek out females and find them by tracing a scent the females emit when ready to mate. However, it is difficult to make general statements about scorpions; in some species females court the males, and in others either sex can begin the mating process. In California Gary Polis studied a species of sand scorpion in which the female initiates courtship. Through the sand she senses vibrations made by a male passing by. Then she makes a series of "mating attacks"—several quick joustlike encounters, followed by retreat, before actual mating begins.

Scorpions mate after an elaborate courtship dance—the *promenade a deux*. The male grasps the female's claws with his and leads her as the pair moves together. In some species the pair seem to be kissing, as the male grasps and nibbles the female's chelicerae—biting mouthparts—with his own.

A pair of scorpions may dance this way for a half hour or more, and promenade for quite a distance over the ground. The goal is to find a hard surface, like a stick or rock, in the right position to enable the pair to mate. The male deposits a sticklike spermatophore (with a small sac of sex cells attached) onto the surface and then drags the female forward so she can take the spermatophore into her reproductive tract.

Throughout the dance and actual mating male scorpions take actions ("kissing," for example) that seem to keep their mates docile. That's because scorpion mating is a risky business: Females often eat their mates.

A male scorpion (left) *grasps the female's claws and leads her in their courtship dance.*

To avoid this fate, males of many species flee as soon as possible after mating. In a species of sand scorpion observed by Gary Polis, immediately after mating "the male violently bats the female with his tail and runs away." Females may scramble off, too, although they are generally larger than their mates and more likely to eat them than to be eaten.

Within a female scorpion the development of the young is more like that of mammals than other arachnids or almost all other animals. Their development (gestation) takes from three to eighteen months. This is longer than many mammals. The longest scorpion gestation periods rival those of such large mammals as sperm whales (sixteen months) and African elephants (twenty-two months).

Scorpions do not lay eggs but give birth to live, large young. The average litter is twenty-five. At birth most young scorpions are enclosed in a membrane. They wriggle free and crawl onto their mother's back. They aren't ready to be independent yet. They are defenseless, with a soft, white outer skeleton, or cuticle. On their

After mating, the female (right) *stung the male and holds him in her claws. She soon ate him.*

mother's back they survive on food reserves from their own bodies and on water that passes up through their mother's cuticle.

A scorpion mother invests a lot of time and energy in her young. She recognizes them by scent. She helps fallen babies to get back up. For a few weeks she is their sanctuary. Then the young molt, breaking out of their old "skins," and emerge with larger, darker, tougher cuticles. (Scorpions molt an average of five times until they reach adult size.) Within a few days, in most species, the young scorpions hop off their mother's back and scatter.

Now the young scorpions are completely independent. They have no further contact with their mother unless they happen to pass near her hideout. This is a reunion to avoid: Good-old-Mom is likely to eat any little scorpions that come along.

In a few species mother scorpions and their young stay together for longer periods. Even after molting the young share their mother's burrow, and sometimes food, for several months. In Brazil both young and mothers of one species work together to dig out living chambers within termite mounds. And on the Ivory Coast of Africa

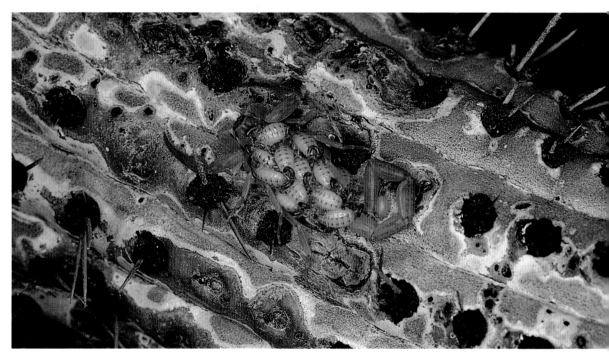

A mother scorpion carries her young on her back until they can survive on their own.

The large emperor scorpion of Africa lives in colonies.

biologists have discovered one scorpion species with an unusual family life. Male and female emperor scorpions, which can reach eight inches in length, live together peacefully and raise their young for two years or longer. The adults catch frogs, mice, and other vertebrates, then rip and chew the food into a soft form for their young.

"This discovery," says Gary Polis, "demonstrates one reason why biologists find scorpions so fascinating. Most scorpions lead solitary lives. They meet only to mate, or to kill. That's generally true, yet now we know that some scorpions cooperate to an unusual degree, living in social colonies.

"How did this behavior develop? Trying to answer such questions is part of the fun of studying scorpions."

THREE

Scorpions of the Dunes

In 1973 Gary Polis began studying scorpions at Windy Point, a large area of dunes in the desert near Palm Springs. At least one night a week for five years he drove from the Riverside campus to Windy Point. There he flicked on the ultraviolet (UV) light and looked for scorpions.

He selected a study area and laid out a grid of seven hundred stakes that were driven into the sand every two meters (about six and a half feet). Each stake had a different number and letter that enabled him to locate the same places—and the same scorpions—again and again. His research was the first intensive study of scorpions in their natural habitat, using UV light.

This light makes scorpions highly visible yet does not disturb them. Black-light bulbs also give off a little non-UV light that helps people see faintly in the dark. On the other hand, UV light can harm human eyes, so scorpion researchers must always wear glasses or safety goggles. The most serious drawback to using UV light in scorpion habitat is the presence of animals that *do not* glow under black light. Rattlesnakes, for instance.

Sidewinders and other rattlesnakes do not glow in ultraviolet light and are a hazard to scorpion studies in the wild.

The Windy Point dunes were home to sidewinders, small rattlesnakes that sometimes rest beneath the sand surface. Once Gary Polis accidentally knelt on a coiled sidewinder partially buried in the sand. "I felt something squishy under my knee. I jumped back hard and landed on a cactus. I ended up with thirty-eight cactus spines in my backside—but no snakebite."

Gary caught some of the sidewinders of Windy Point and sprayed fluorescent paint on their backs so they would glow under UV light if he encountered them again. He also began wearing snake chaps made of woven brass wire and urged his companions to do the same. One of his assistants was saved from a sidewinder's fangs when the snake struck her chaps.

To follow the lives of individual scorpions, Gary caught nearly a thousand and gave each one an identifying mark, made on its back with little dots of different-colored paint. (On adults the marks last several years. Young scorpions shed their special marks when they molt and new paint had to be put on their new cuticles.) In the process he became adept at picking up scorpions with his bare fingers. Though it is possible to safely pick up a scorpion this way, Gary recommends using long forceps. Fluorescent paint on the tips of the forceps helps a researcher pick up scorpions swiftly and safely.

Four scorpion species lived on the desert sands of Windy Point. Two were small and the third was the largest species in North America, the hairy scorpion, which grows up to six inches long. The fourth species present was the sand scorpion, *Paruroctonus*

By marking scorpions with paint Gary Polis was able to recognize individuals and learn about their travels and longevity.

mesaensis, which measures about three inches long. It dominated the area, making up 95 percent of all scorpions.

The females of all four species gave birth in midsummer, and the young grew at about the same pace. This made it easy to tell a scorpion's age by its size. Gary divided the sand scorpion population into three age classes: young (under one year), intermediate (one to two years), and adult (two to six years).

"What I found," Gary Polis wrote in the July 1989 issue of *Natural History* magazine, "was that the three age groups of sand scorpions are as different from one another—in ecology and behavior—as if they were different species. They capture different prey, suffer different predators, emerge to the surface from the burrows at different times of the night and year, and occupy different microhabitats."

Gary usually found sand scorpions within a few feet of their burrows. Commonly they were hidden inside their burrows, which they had dug at thirty- to forty-five-degree angles to the sand surface. He saw individual marked scorpions at the surface on only one-fifth to one-half of all possible nights. Even then they stayed above ground only a few hours.

Gary Polis concluded, "Individuals of this species remain in their burrows for 92 to 97 percent of their existence. The burrow is the location for almost all normal activities of burrowing scorpions: birth, maternal care, molting, even mating."

Burrow scorpions do leave home to catch food and usually eat it above ground. During his five-year study, Gary Polis witnessed sixteen hundred instances of sand scorpions eating their prey.

Tree-dwelling scorpions and some other species actively hunt for food but burrowing species are sit-and-wait or ambush predators. They emerge from their burrows and wait motionless near the entrance. They often wait a long time before a moth flies over-

A female sand scorpion of the species Paruroctonus mesaensis *that was most abundant on the Windy Point dunes.*

head or other prey passes nearby. Once a scorpion detects an insect or other prey, it runs to the animal and seizes it. If the prey is large or struggles a lot the scorpion quickly quells it with a paralyzing sting. Other prey is simply held by the scorpion's claws. Still alive, it is chewed a bit, then digested by enzymes that the scorpion pours out. The victim's soft parts become a soupy liquid that the scorpion sucks into its stomach. The meal often lasts several hours.

Scorpions eat just about anything they can catch, hold, and digest. The sand scorpions of Windy Point ate spiders, many kinds of insects, and other scorpions. In other habitats, scorpions may eat snails, earthworms, and centipedes. The biggest scorpions sometimes kill geckos, lizards, mice, and other small vertebrates.

Scorpions themselves are prey for many animals, ranging in size from spiders to coyotes. Owls and bats swoop to grab scorpions at night; lizards and some snakes hunt them by day. Southwestern scorpions are frequent meals for burrowing owls and grasshopper

26

A sand scorpion eating a trap-door spider (left) *and another* (below) *with a sphinx moth it captured.*

mice. Before dining some predators bite off or break off a scorpion's tail to avoid being stung.

Adult male scorpions are hardest hit by predators. They abandon their burrows during the mating season and may travel long distances in search of mates. At Windy Point Gary Polis measured distances covered by male sand scorpions. Some traveled more than seventy-five feet in a half hour and three hundred thirty feet in a night.

The males he observed weren't very active on moonlit nights, when they would be more easily seen by predators. Still, any scorpion far from its burrow or other hideout is in danger. Some roving males are killed by predators; some may die of starvation or high temperatures. The greatest threat, however, is other scorpions. Even before a male scorpion finds a female and risks being eaten by her after mating, it runs a gauntlet of other scorpions waiting for a meal.

"When I began studying scorpions at Windy Point," Gary Polis says, "I never dreamed that a major part of my research would be cannibalism. But I saw scorpions killing and eating other scorpions, including their own kind, hundreds of times."

Writing in *Natural History* magazine, Gary Polis explained why scorpions are so prone to eat one another: "Smaller individuals, regardless of species, count as nothing more than a potential meal for bigger ones. And in a fight between scorpions, size is all-important. During a fight each combatant grasps the tail of the other with its pincers, attempting to fend off the deadly stinger. Inevitably the larger individual, able to exert more leverage with its tail, manages to insert its paralyzing stinger."

All species are vulnerable when young and small. Early in its life, for instance, a hairy scorpion—largest in North America—is easy prey for medium-sized and adult sand scorpions. When the surviving hairy scorpions grow up, however, "the tables turn, and they often capture and eat all sizes of sand scorpions."

At certain times of the year Gary Polis found that up to half of all prey caught by sand scorpions were other scorpions. Many were fellow sand scorpions. "This cannibalism is so intense," he wrote, "it appears to limit the population of sand scorpions."

Facts like these about scorpion ecology were reported in Gary's doctoral thesis, which he completed in 1977. After graduating from the University of California at Riverside, Gary became an assistant professor in the Department of Zoology at Oregon State University and taught courses in animal behavior and population ecology. His curiosity about scorpions remained strong. He made frequent trips to California, trying to learn more about dune scorpions.

In 1978 Gary Polis, shown with his father, earned a doctoral degree from the University of California for his scorpion research.

A sand scorpion feasts on one of the smaller species in its habitat.

His research on these scorpions continued even after 1979, when he became an assistant professor of biology at Vanderbilt University in Tennessee. At Vanderbilt he taught courses and also guided the research of graduate students, several of whom investigated scorpions. Every summer he headed west to the Palm Springs area, gathering more information about dune scorpions. He was especially interested in their predation on one another.

He wondered what effect sand scorpions had on the two smaller species of their dune habitat. To find out he marked off three hundred study areas, each a hundred meters square (one hundred twenty square yards). Over a thirty-month period he removed more than six thousand sand scorpions from these areas and watched to see whether this affected the numbers of the two smaller species. The results were dramatic: One species became about one-and-a-half times more abundant, the other became six times more abundant.

Their numbers had been kept in check by sand scorpion predation, not by lack of food or some other factor. The feasting of scorpions on one another, Gary Polis concluded, is a major factor in deciding where they live and how many there are.

FOUR

Adventures and Misadventures

When you are looking for scorpions on a pitch-black night it is good to have companions along. They can carry gear and help take verbal notes with a tape recorder, a necessary tool, since the light of a flashlight scares scorpions. They can help listen for the hiss of a rattlesnake.

Through the years, Gary Polis has shared desert nights with friends and graduate students. His wife, Sharon, whom he married in 1985, has helped with his research, as have his brothers Dan and Steve.

Gary winces when he remembers all the work that went into one study in the Palm Springs area. In order to learn more about scorpion predation, he carefully planned experiments that involved building large enclosures in the desert. To avoid vandalism the enclosures were built in a protected area. It had no sand and, since sand-burrowing scorpions were to be used in the experiments, several truckloads of sand were brought in. To make sure the scorpions could burrow deep enough, the desert soil was rototilled, then the sand was spread over the surface.

Sharon Polis sometimes helps Gary with his research. Their son, Evan, is on the right. Sharon and Gary show the gear needed for night studies: ultraviolet bulbs in lanterns, glasses to protect their eyes from UV light, and boots and chaps for defense against poisonous snakes.

All of this work was done by Gary, his wife Sharon, brothers Dan and Steve, and his research associate Sharon McCormick. They often labored in 105-degree heat. Next they built the enclosures with walls of aluminum sheeting. Now they were ready to release two species of scorpions into the enclosures. They had searched the desert for several weeks in order to collect about eighty individuals of a small, uncommon species. The second, larger species was more easily collected.

At last the night came for releasing the scorpions in their enclosures. "Within thirty minutes," Gary recalls, "I noticed a small scorpion had escaped from its enclosure. It climbed right up the aluminum walls. I knew that the big species couldn't do that but had never thought of seeing whether the little one could. Thanks to this oversight, the experiments could not be done. All of our work was wasted except, perhaps, for one benefit: I always tell my students about this project, and maybe it helps them plan their research more carefully."

Dan and Steve continue to help at Gary's main area of scorpion research, the Mexican peninsula called Baja California and nearby islands in the Gulf of California. Gary began to explore Baja in the late 1970s and has focused more and more of his research effort there. Rugged, wild, with very little water, Baja California is a paradise for scorpions—and for people who study them. Gary Polis explained why: "The scorpion fauna of Baja California is the most **diverse** in the world, with a total of sixty-one species; in any one **area**, up to thirteen may occur together."

One Baja species that lives along the high-tide mark of beaches **holds** the world record for population density. "In any square meter **of shore** habitat, you may find between two and a dozen of these

The rugged desert habitat of Mexico's Baja California is home to sixty-one scorpion species.

scorpions. It is not a good place to spread your sleeping bag," Gary remarked.

On many of the smaller islands there are no large land predators. Scorpions, spiders, and lizards are plentiful, and a wealth of animal and plant food washes up from the sea. This situation, with sea and desert-island habitats side by side, intrigues Gary Polis. He is studying the relationships between scorpions, spiders, and lizards.

Each summer he is helped by volunteers from Earthwatch, an organization that matches researchers with people who want to support research with work and money. The volunteers visit more than thirty islands, surveying animal life and sometimes collecting lizards and spiders.

Not all of Gary's research involves scorpions: "They figure in my work a lot because of the habitats and the questions I find fascinating. I'm basically an ecologist who concentrates on scorpions because I love the information they can give me."

In 1988 Gary began visiting the Namib Desert of southwestern Africa, another area rich in scorpions. Among the forty-five species there, some live on trees, with as many as fifty individuals in a single tree. The scorpions share the tree habitat with a single species of spider, and Gary is studying the relationships between the different predators.

The Namib Desert is rich in poisonous animals. They include cobras, adders, two kinds of deadly scorpions, and one of the most lethal spiders on earth. Gary was especially cautious there in 1993, when he was accompanied by Sharon and their three-year-old son, Evan.

Research in wild places can be risky. One summer night in 1986, Gary and graduate student Denise Due were taken by boat to explore an island in the Gulf of California. The boat's pilot was inexperienced, and they worried about the return trip across a

This pilot whale, dead from a shark bite, washed up on a Baja California beach. Scorpions prey upon insects and crustaceans that feed on such carcasses.

passageway the Mexicans call the Channel of Little Hell.

A storm blew in, and the channel was a raging sea. Partway across, the boat's motor failed. The pilot had no tools aboard. As heavy seas threatened to swamp the boat, Gary used a pocketknife to get the motor going. They reached shore safely. He says, however, that this near-disaster caused his hair to start turning gray.

In 1988 Gary was a passenger in a van that rolled over on an isolated dirt road in Namibia. His foot was crushed and both bones in his lower right leg were snapped. Medical treatment was several hours away. As it turned out, the treatment was also flawed. After his leg had healed for a month he learned that the bones had not been set right. He had several operations, including a bone trans-

A tree scorpion of the Namib Desert, photographed on an acacia tree under ultraviolet light.

plant, and wore a brace for two years. Now one leg is a bit shorter than the other, and he no longer plays much of his favorite sport, basketball. Still, he plays volleyball and racquetball.

The injury did not reduce his passion for learning about scorpions and desert ecology. He edited a newly published book, *The Ecology of Desert Communities,* and he and a colleague are writing a book about the natural history of Baja California. Understanding deserts and their life is important, Gary says, because deserts are expanding on several continents. In Mexico and the Southwestern United States, overgrazing by cattle changes rangeland to desert.

The study of scorpions seems weird to some people, but Gary Polis quickly gives four reasons why such research, and scorpions themselves, are valuable. In many ways scorpions are ideal research animals, in the wild or in laboratories. For example, Gary explains, "Because a scorpion's nervous system is so simple, it produces an excellent general model for studying how behavior and the nervous system work."

Scorpions already contribute to human health. Study of scorpion venom led to the development of a drug for treating strokes, the sudden attacks that can leave people paralyzed. Scientists expect that scorpion poisons will yield other useful drugs and perhaps chemicals that kill harmful insects.

People visiting deserts seldom see scorpions. They see lizards, ground squirrels, and coyotes and assume that such vertebrates are the most important animals. In some deserts, however, scorpions are so plentiful that they outweigh all of the vertebrates combined.

Gary Polis in Africa.

As successful predators they play major roles in the ecology of deserts.

Finally, Gary Polis says, "Scorpions are simply interesting in themselves. With their long gestation, live birth, and long lives they are more like mammals than other arachnids. Though all scorpions are alike in some ways, there is also great variety among the fifteen hundred species—and hundreds more will probably be discovered. Sure, they may be ugly and nasty by human standards, but they are also fascinating."

Listening to Gary Polis talk about scorpions and his research, people often begin to feel differently about them. Try this: Imagine you are in the scene that began this book. You are standing in a wild desert. Overhead, the constellation called Scorpio and other stars provide the only light. You are alone, surrounded by scorpions.

What a delightful place to be!

FURTHER READING

The single most valuable information source on scorpions is *The Biology of Scorpions*, edited by Gary Polis. This book and several chapters from it are among the sources cited below.

Angier, Natalie. "The Scorpion, Bizarre and Nasty, Recruits New Admirers." *The New York Times*, November 27, 1990.

Brownell, P. H. "Prey Detection by the Sand Scorpion." *Scientific American*, June 1984, 86–97.

Cloudsley-Thompson, J. L. "Scorpions in Mythology, Folklore, and History." In *The Biology of Scorpions*, edited by Gary Polis. Stanford: Stanford University Press, 1990.

Polis, Gary, editor. *The Biology of Scorpions*. Stanford, California: Stanford University Press, 1990.

Polis, Gary. "The Unkindest Sting of All." *Natural History*, July 1989, 34–39.

Polis, Gary. "Why I Love Scorpions." *Boys' Life*, August 1992, 10–13.

Polis, Gary, and W. David Sissom. "Life History." In *The Biology of Scorpions*, edited by Gary Polis. Stanford: Stanford University Press, 1990.

Warburg, Michael, and Gary Polis. "Behavioral Responses, Rhythms, and Activity Patterns." In *The Biology of Scorpions*, edited by Gary Polis. Stanford: Stanford University Press, 1990.

INDEX

595.4   Pringle, Laurence
PRI
         Scorpion man

                        CM-52601

$15.95

DATE			
Colluk			
OC 25 '95			
Gartner			
NV 8 '96			